For Frankie, Billy and Ged
AG

For Grandma and Grandpa
Scarborough, with love
CW

Text copyright © 2001 by Adèle Geras
Illustrations copyright © 2001 by Catherine Walters
All rights reserved.

CIP Data is available.

Published in the United States 2001 by Dutton Children's Books,
a division of Penguin Putnam Books for Young Readers
345 Hudson Street, New York, New York 10014
www.penguinputnam.com

Originally published in Great Britain 2001 by Little Tiger Press,
an imprint of Magi Publications, London
Typography by Richard Amari
Printed in Belgium
First American Edition
ISBN 0-525-46771-8
2 4 6 8 10 9 7 5 3 1

Sleep Tight, Ginger Kitten

by Adèle Geras

illustrated by

Catherine Walters

DUTTON CHILDREN'S BOOKS
New York

Ginger Kitten
has one white paw
and a small white
spot in the
center of his face.
Today he is looking for
a napping place....

Ginger Kitten
likes to run
and jump
and crawl
and leap.

But most of all,
he likes to sleep.

First Ginger Kitten
tries a wooden chair.
It's much too hard.
He can't sleep there.

Ginger Kitten crawls
behind the bathroom door,
where he can't be seen.

He washes his paws
and when they're clean…

He snuggles into the
kitten-shaped nook.
But Daddy opens the door,
pushing it into
his little face.
This spot isn't cozy
anymore.
So out he dashes
across the floor.

Next, Ginger Kitten
finds a box.
He pushes and squishes,
but it's much too small.

Quickly, he spots

the mat in the hall.

He stretches out
his two front feet.
Abracadabra,
there are his claws!
Scritch! Scratch!
Ginger Kitten
loves doing that.
Then carefully
he rests his head,
but the mat is too prickly
to make a nice bed.

Upstairs he leaps on a softer bed
and finds a toy to chew.

Almost comfortable...
until Mommy says "Shoo!"

He tries the closet next
but bumps his head
on the hanging clothes.
The floor is covered
with pairs of shoes.
This isn't a place where
a kitten can snooze!

One last try—into the den
Ginger Kitten tiptoes.

There's someone on the sofa—
someone he knows.

Ginger Kitten
jumps up and purrs
on the child's warm lap.

Finally, he's found
the perfect place
for a nap!